PSYCHOTIC
INTERLUDE

Toneye Eyenot

Cover Art and Design by: Mar Garcia-Amorena - The Bold Mom / Disturbing Drawings©

Foreword

Welcome back to the darkness of my mind(s). If you are new to my twisted musings, there are no apologies made here. You will be disturbed, you will be dismayed. There are things you will not be able to unsee, perturbed feelings which will stay with you long after you put this book down. Tales of sadism, of calculating killers, the darkest desperations of the human spirit leading to the most corrupted and malevolent of actions.

Psychopaths…Human Monsters – Nobody is immune. Nobody is truly safe.

Enjoy this spiralling descent into your very own PSYCHOTIC INTERLUDE.

Let's begin with an experiment, shall we? This is as much an experiment for me as it is for you, dear reader. Eye would like to challenge you to completely and sensorially immerse yourself in the experience of this poor, hapless victim; from that very first moment of realisation that you're in some deadly serious trouble, to your final, spluttering breath...and even beyond.

My challenge is to be equally as difficult. Eye intend to take you there and keep you, ensnared in terror's enthrallment; no matter how much you squirm in discomfort or wish to look away. You are my prisoner and it is my challenge to fill your soul with as real a fear as eye can summon; to give you no hope of escape.

Let's begin...

An Experiment in Fear

Put yourself in the picture. No, come on now, humour me and *put yourself fully in the scenario.* Your arm is being broken. Snapped at the elbow by powerful hands; hands which extinguish any hope of being released.

I'm not talking about the sudden, violent kind of break either. The man (or monster, if you will) who has you at his terrifying absence of mercy, sits on your back as you lay prostrate in the dirt, your right arm stretched out, straight and taut in his vice grip.

At its fullest extension, and with his nightmare voice drifting around your ears, informing you of the slow and agonising process of your impending death, the burn of muscles stretched to beyond their capacity is merely the introduction to a universe of pain.

This man intends to break you, limb by limb and oh, so slowly.

Build a back catalogue now in your mind. A recounting of every fright and fear you have experienced throughout your life; from the most trivial, to what you had previously considered soul destroying and life ruining, then roll them all into one big ball of fear.

All of those fears you have endured and subsequently carried with you throughout your life, even those that had at the time seemed so real and devastating, were all unfounded. Fear of the unknown and nothing more. You are still here, right? Then what were you afraid of? This?

Well, ok, that's fair enough, but your lifetime's worth of fear you have just recalled and neatly bundled is still only an empty husk next to what you are experiencing now. *This* is fear. True, real and entirely validated fear.

Now, you are face down, in a quiet, deserted place which swallows your screams into a vacuous, uncaring oblivion… and you are alone with *him*. His sadistic narrative places your fears in the undeniable realm of the 'known'. You are going to die, but it will not be as simple as just having your candle snuffed out. This is going to take some time, and the worst pain imaginable…beginning Now.

Adrenaline is making your heart ache, with the frantic pounding that accompanies your predicament. You tell yourself many things, all of which you know won't come to pass, but of course, you must cling to that tiny sliver of hope.

Somebody will come to your rescue… Yeah, right. Nobody comes here. You have always loved the solitude and peace. The entire reason why this has been your favourite place to come to for such a long time. Ironic, don't you think?

You can't die now; not like this! Sure, you can. What makes you any different from any other victim of torture and brutal murder? It happens every day, somewhere in the world. Right now, somebody somewhere is being tortured mercilessly, with no regard to the sanctity of life.

There are some evil people in this world of ours, and there is no shortage of victims, among whose ranks you have now joined.

Stress is increased on your elbow slowly, as your muscles and ligaments begin to tear. The bloodcurdling screams of cinema's greatest scream queens sound like soothing morning birdsong, in comparison to the horrible noise that escapes your lungs. Yes, this is what a *real* scream of agony sounds like.

The sound, not unlike plastic bubble packaging being mashed under water, of your tendons and ligaments stretched beyond their limits to ripping, makes you vomit in pain.

The white noise in your skull dulls the din of your screaming to the background, and you feel you are about to pass out. You can't struggle, or wrench yourself free, no matter your hunger for survival. All the fight has been crushed out of you. Your assailant is far too strong and too heavy to resist.

SNAP!

Your elbow joint is loose but still attached. The extreme pressure applied to your outstretched arm was such that your ulna has splintered and become deformed, but your radius has snapped in two and now tears through the flesh of your forearm as a jagged, meaty white protuberance.

By instinct, to escape this unnatural agony, you fall unconscious for what seems to you, only mere milliseconds.

You are torn cruelly from your sanctuary of unconsciousness, by three fingers in each corner of your mouth. The sensitive flesh of your lips begins to split, as the beast on your back slowly pulls your mouth into an involuntary grin of death.

You are awakened by the sound of your own horrid screams. You are the star of your very own show here. He wouldn't have you slumber through the juicy scenes of such a masterpiece of horror.

Frantically, you grab at his fingers with your left hand, as the split in your top lip opens wider, tearing up to your septum. Tears and dirt mix to form an irritating layer over each eyeball, leaving you blinded, and with every other sense maddeningly heightened. The world you know is reduced to the confines of this nightmare experience, from which you have no hope of waking.

The steel trap fingers release your torn, bloody mouth and catch your wildly grasping hand. His knee digs into your elbow, pinning your arm to the ground. Taking your thumb in one hand, your little finger in the other, he violently begins yanking them apart.

Your thumb is first to pop from its joint, immediately followed by your finger giving way at the second knuckle.

In desperation, you try to reach for his hands with your useless, broken arm. Fresh agony surges through your entire being. Your mangled right arm dragging across the rough dirt only mere inches, before the briefly lost memory of its devastation pounds a violent reminder like a mallet to your heart. The webbing between thumb and forefinger tears, and with one final tug, your thumb is snapped and wrenched free from your hand.

You feel like a helpless insect in the deliberate hands of a sadistic child, curiously plucking wings and legs to see how much you can endure before you perish. Indeed, you wonder how much longer before you die and can finally be free of this terminal session of torture? At this stage, you are already beginning to acquiesce to the notion of Death. The unspeakable agony seems commonplace now. As though this agony is all you have ever known.

In your delirium, you ponder the distinct possibility that you've died already and this is Hell, in which case, the end has already passed and you have entered into a new beginning – a beginning devoid of any end. Renewed terror permeates your mind at this prospect, along with a fresh onslaught of pain. He has much yet to accomplish in his quest for your supreme disfigurement.

He is slow, deliberate and methodical in his execution. His tools of torture; naught but his bare hands. Your dismembered thumb pokes against your cheek as he goes to work on the rest of your fingers, bending and twisting them individually, this way and that until they break, while your howls of agony continue.

He shifts his weight on your back, allowing you the briefest unencumbered inhalation. Your lungs swell gratefully with the previously sparse oxygen, only to be inundated with the dust of the ground you are pinned to. A coughing fit ensues, which immediately becomes a suffocating choke, as he settles once again atop you. Pressing his foot down hard on your forearm, he takes your mangled hand in his and begins to slowly twist it counter-clockwise.

The power and strength of this man seems

inhuman. Every touch is like a hammer blow; each grip is crushing – but his voice... his voice, and the words that roll off his tongue like venomous, malicious demons, to stab at your ears in a constant reminder of the inevitable.

You are unable to scream now, as your lungs burn with dust and dirt. All you can manage are feeble, gasping chokes and gags. All the while, your wrist is turned in his powerful grip. The carpal bones of your hand are crushed, tendons, veins and arteries severed, as your hand swells with blood, yet still he keeps turning.

Releasing his foot from your arm, he continues twisting your hand until it snaps from the scaphoid bone of your wrist. You gag so violently that you vomit profusely, and then, with lungs debilitated and on fire, you fall back into the sweet respite of unconsciousness once again, if only for the briefest of moments.

His knee falls heavily in the centre of your left forearm, jolting you back to the waking nightmare. Squeezing his massive hand around your twisted, broken paw, he pulls your arm up, intent on breaking it. You kick and struggle violently to no avail. You are thrust deep into the heart of this new level of excruciating agony; a bewildering and frantic realm inside your mind that has you in its torturous embrace, with no intention of letting go. Your ability to scream has all but left you, though if you were able, you surely would. You can barely even breathe.

You are now yearning for what you have feared most, but Death does not heed your internal pleas. It hovers patiently over you, in the form of this sadistic creature, and simply witnesses through *his* eyes, your torturous and gradual end without sympathy or empathy.

The waking nightmare continues, with the swollen, tenderised flesh of your wrist splitting and tearing, blood spraying as the pressure is released and your mangled hand is removed from limb.

Taking your hand, he digs the splintered, exposed bone of your forefinger into your sinus cavity and proceeds to plough your eyeball from its socket. Your head pulled back, with your fringe bunched in his grip until you feel your trachea rupturing, your eyeball dislodges to hang down your cheek.

Tossing your hand aside, and with your head still pulled back to its absolute limit, he reaches his other hand around to grasp your jaw. Pulling down, you feel it begin to unhinge from your skull. With a vicious sideways jerk, the jaw snaps with a deafening crack. Searing hot pain shoots up the back of your skull, and it would seem, Death has taken mercy on your suffering.

Unintentionally, the beast dominating your broken, helpless body has disengaged your cervical vertebra, snapping your neck. Yet, in your final moments of life, a new fear engulfs your fading cognizance.

Your life flashes before your mind's eye, in a cinematic display of all of your misdeeds and transgressions. You were never religious. You found prayer to be pointless and a precious waste of time. Still, the dominant societal conditioning of what, or who is 'God' now takes governance of your awareness. Your time on this earth has come to pass, but… Where will you be going now?

This one may raise a few hackles – pull a few triggers, but as the foreword expressed, there are no apologies made. In a society burdened with countless rules and pointless laws, one is left to wonder; is common sense even a thing anymore? Why do we need to be told how to live, as long as we're not harming anyone in the process? Why do we go through our lives, content and happy with this insidious form of slavery? Sure, there are some people who are inherently stupid and have no concept of right or wrong, but do the rest of us have to suffer for it? The only rule to me which makes perfect sense, is "Don't Be A Cunt". Anything outside of that is, as they say, tyranny and oppression – an indoctrination beginning from the moment we become aware of our surroundings and ending when we take that final dirt nap. It's enough to bring on one of those 'psychotic interludes', don't ya reckon?

This disturbing tale appeared in the anthology, 'FUCK THE RULES' by Leviathan – an imprint of Great British Horror

https://www.amazon.com/Fuck-Rules-Richard-Chizmar-ebook/dp/B074TS7HG9/

Don't Be a Cunt (The Only Rule to Follow)

What a piece of shit world we live in, where one has to pay to wake up. Taxed from the moment you switch on a light because it's stupid o'clock in the fucking morning, it's still dark outside and will be for at least another hour and a half, and you have to stumble around like a zombie to get ready for work.

Work…what the fuck is that about anyway? I'll tell ya. It's about draggin' your arse outta bed five days a week, goin' to a place you hate bein' at and slavin' your guts out for eight hours a day to make some fat, greedy cunt rich off the sweat of your labours. And that's not even the worst part. Two days out of those five, you do all of this for free! That's right, fucking free!

There's that dreaded 'T' word again. That's the percentage of your time and hard-earned pittance goin' to the Taxman. Never thought about that, did ya? No, because all you can think about is makin' it to your next paycheck without snappin' and smashin' the boss's smug face through his mahogany desk. Isn't that just enough to make you say, '*fuck this shit,*

17

I'm gonna start killin' cunts if this continues much longer'?

You're a slave. Blundering your way around this free-range prison we call 'society', under the illusion that you're free. You are not free. Don't fuckin' kid yourself, mate. None of us are free. We're the bottom feeders, consuming the excrement of our 'betters', who in turn are consuming the excrement of their betters and so on and so on, all the way up the shit smeared ladder to *success* – a word only a very select few ever truly manage to grasp the concept of.

If success is measured by hard work and perseverance, then shouldn't we all be succeeding? By rights, yes, we should be…but we aren't. We're trapped in and endless cycle of 'sleep, wake up, work, consume, sleep, wake up, work, consume' until ya eventually get to retire with fuckall time and fuckall money left to reap any significant reward for a life of toil.

All I can say is, thank fuck they abolished the carbon tax. Think about that for a moment. It's fine if you wanna inhale, but in order to carry on livin' you need to exhale, and to exhale, they expect you to pay a tax for that? A tax to fucking breathe? Come on! How much more can they squeeze out of us before there's simply nothin' left?

Getting' to ya, aren't I. I can see that vein throb, the spastic twitch in your eye as I slowly drag you outta the fugue you've lived your entire life in. Those fucks who sit in their ivory towers, making up rules and laws to dictate how you live your life – the untouchables – laugh with abandon at the billions of performing monkeys under their control.

I know you. You're a decent person and try to do right by everyone – a noble trait. What do ya get in return though? Gratitude? Yeah, from some. Most, however, are caught up in their own fugue and overlook the efforts of their fellow man. Society has become so numb, so…selfish. It's not their fault. They are just like you; just trying to get by in an increasingly hostile world.

But to protect themselves from being exposed, these secretive demons who pull our strings divert our attention from their nefarious doings and cast it onto others like yourself. Your hatred, your anger, your fucking furious rage, if combined with the rage of seven billion others, would bring those ivory towers crashing to the ground faster than the World Trade Centre. Divide and conquer; that's the age-old game they play.

While you get shuffled around on the game board of life, obeying your invisible masters – teachers, the judicial system, law enforcement…. fuckin' God – you have been taught to hate people you don't even know, based on nothing more than a label. Religion, social status, political persuasion, you name it; they are nothing more than systems of control designed to keep you docile while you stuff your face on toxic garbage packaged as food, and cheer for your favourite, grossly overpaid football team on the idiot box.

All the while, throughout all these myriad of carefully orchestrated distractions, those men in their ivory towers hatch foul plots against us.

That's it. Now you're gettin' it. I see that spark in your eye, now let it ignite. Know your enemy and don't let 'em tell ya what to fuckin' do anymore. This is your life and yours alone, so live and die on your terms, not theirs. Fuck their rules because the only rule which holds any validity is '*don't be a cunt*'; everything else is tyranny and oppression, inflicted upon you by, yep…cunts.

PINNNNGGGGGGG!

Welcome to your epiphany.

I'm glad you've finally understood and taken heed. I am your voice of reason and let me tell you, after all these decades in your numb skull, watchin' you, through your clouded eyes, bowin' to your masters and demandin' homage from your peers like a good little slave, there have been times I've wanted to walk you out into traffic, off a cliff, into that woodchipper in the lumberyard you've slaved at for the past twenty five years.

Whichever method, ending your miserable existence would've been a pleasing respite because I don't think I could've taken much more of your blind ignorance. You are better than that.

So, are ya just gonna keep on sittin' here? Let's go! It's time to fight back. Time to fuck the system that's been fuckin' you nine ways from Sunday since ya left the womb. I know just the place to start – where it all started with you…TV. This was where your indoctrination began, where you were first exposed to the insidious art of distraction. Your parents weren't to know that when they would plonk you down on the floor in front of the idiot box so you'd be quiet and out of the way, they were pluggin' you into the matrix.

Your sledgehammer in the shed will take care of the immediate problem, and then we can move onto the bigger 'picture' – the local broadcasting station.

That's it, take a swing...WAIT! Unplug it from the wall first, you idiot. You wanna electrocute yourself? That'll bring things to an untimely end. It's great to see ya so enthusiastic, but geez.

I have to prepare you for the fact that people are gonna die. It's a necessary evil though. Don't feel bad. They have been complicit in dispensing the materials – the mind poison – which has helped to keep you docile and subservient to a bullshit agenda.

From the deceptively named *reality* shows which dominate television *programming*, interspersed with blatant as well as subliminal advertisements to make you feel you need things which are useless, to the worst of all…the *news* reports; so embellished of the truth and grossly sensationalised to evoke the desired emotional response. They have been brainwashing you your entire life. Fuck them. They are parasites and need to be eradicated.

You feel better, yeah? Feels good to destroy something that has ruled your life. Trust me, this is nothing compared to what you will feel when you are finally free. Tip of the iceberg right here. It's 1AM and the cleaner down at the TV station will be finishing his shift in half an hour. You ready? Let's do this.

You wanna arrive before he leaves, so you can easily gain access, and it's gonna take at least fifteen minutes to get there. After that, you'll have about four hours to completely destroy the place before the puppets turn up for the day's puppet show. Grab your hoodie and a bandana to wrap around your face. You'll be on camera…at least until ya take 'em out… hehe.

***

You're drivin' like an old bitch, put ya foot

down, for fuck's sake. There's nobody on the road at this hour; fuck the speed limit. That's just another bullshit rule. You're a competent driver. As long as you drive safely, you can go as fast as ya damn well please. Red light? Run the cunt. Red – a colour known to promote irritability and increase rage. Why the fuck do they make a stop light red? I don't give a fuck how they try to explain that one away or justify it. How many people enjoy coming to a red light? Fuckin' no one.

Here we are, pull up over there, outta sight.

Now we wait. Yeah, sometimes when ya decide to fuck the rules, there's a little waitin' involved if ya wanna do it right. You timed it well though. He should be comin' out in a few minutes. See? If you'd stuck to the limit and waited at that red light, chances are you'd have turned up too late.

That must be his car over there. It's a pretty lit up area of the carpark…how's your throwin' arm? C'mon, let's do this. You have a few minutes, tops. Grab some rocks from around that garden and take out those lights, quick. May as well take 'em all out while you're at it. Plunge the whole exterior into darkness; it'll be harder for you to get spotted.

Niiiice! You're a fuckin' natural, mate. Alright, gonna spring this one on ya so don't freak out and bail on me. You're gonna have to kill this cunt. Bein' your voice of reason, there's a good chance I'm gonna fade into your subconscious for a spell while reason takes a back seat. Shit's gonna get messy and more than a little chaotic, but I have faith in ya. You can do this. Just think of him as a TV set as ya bash his brains in.

I'm only sayin' this because you'll need his keys and the security code to get in without settin' off the alarm. Just break his leg at first. You're gonna need him to turn off the alarm, and then fuck him; he'll have outgrown his usefulness. Kill the cunt because if ya don't, he'll squeal, and the pigs'll be here before ya get a chance to destroy much of anything. We've got a lot more to do after this.

Yeah yeah, I know. 'Don't be a cunt'. Think of it this way: Y'know the saying – *to make an omelette, ya gotta break a few eggs* – well, as rough as it might sound, this cleaner is just an egg and you have one helluva big omelette to make. Chalk it up to collateral damage and try not to think about it too hard. You've got this, mate.

Quick, hide! Here he comes. Remember, the crowbar will probably kill him straight up if ya hit him in the head and we don't want that. Not yet anyway. Just aim for the knee, but be prepared to shut him up real quick because that fucker is gonna scream like a bitch.

Don't chicken out on me now. Damn, your heart is beatin' fast! Stay with me, man. The blood poundin' in your ears is fuckin' loud. You'll wanna be able to hear what I'm sayin'. Just stay here behind the car until he gets to his door. Ready? Ready? …….. OK, Now!

Shut him up! Shut him the fuck up! He's gonna scream the whole fuckin' neighbourhood down. Shove that glove in his trap. That's the way. Ah shit, man, that even made me cringe. That's no easy feat either. Nicely done. Time for Mr. Cleanerman to go back to work. Double shift for this fucker.

Pick his keys up, you're gonna need that swipe card. Get him up, let's go. If he won't – or can't walk, fuckin' drag him. Threaten to take out his other leg.

***

We're in, alarm disarmed, now fuck him up. Just one to the h...ok, two. Or three...four. He's dead, man. You can stop now. Fuck, mate. You like this a little too much. Remember, don't be a cunt. We're here to destroy this place and time's a tickin'. Let's start with takin' out that camera. You're covered up pretty well but you never know these days. Don't forget your glove. No fingerprints. Right, we have a few hours to play, let's see how much damage you can do.

Ah, the TV Production Studio...so this is where the *magic* happens. Where they manipulate footage to suit whatever agenda they wish to push on the gullible population. Smash it all, room by room. A crowbar is such a versatile tool, don't ya think? Nice work, mate. You're really gettin' the hang of this. You have a nice smile when you're enjoyin' yourself. You should enjoy yourself more often hahaha. Leave it; you've done sufficient damage here.

There's so much more to see.

The studio floor: here is where the actors play their role. So much to see here, all of which is manufactured – fake. Start with their precious green screen. Destroy that shit, their treasured tool of deception. All these cameras, stage lighting rigs, video monitors…smash 'em and then we'll move on to the control room for the final blow.

Well, this'll be easy. Wait, do you smell smoke? Looks like you've started a fire back there in the studio. Well, well, well! Things just got even easier! Quick, into the Master Control Room for a speedy rampage – just for good measure – and then you're outta here. You can let the fire do the rest. I suspect fire alarms will be goin' off any minute now.

Make sure you smash that panel there good 'n' proper. That's the sprinkler system. Can't have that undoin' all your hard work now. Poor ol' Cleanerman will be burnt to a crisp; might even be burnt beyond any sign of foul play on your part. OK, let's get outta here.

***

Now, tell me that wasn't fun, yeah? Liberating, innit? Ah, don't feel bad for the egg. Your omelette is startin' to take form and you wanna be able to enjoy a good meal when this is all over.

Now I'm gonna let ya think for yourself. After all, this is what it's all about. So, you started out on the road to your enslavement as a very young boy, having the teLIEvision slowly brainwash ya into subservience. What came next? School, yeah, but there was something before that – c'mon, think… Fuckin' Hell, do I have to spell it out for ya? Think! I just gave you a clue right there. No, not spell; sounds like, though. *Hell*, goooood. And where do we get the rikokulous notion of this imaginary place? You guessed it, buddy. You're goin' to church hahahahaha.

You probably don't remember this; it was such a long time ago, but when you were just a wee sprog, your parents took ya to one of these houses of lies and had some sick mother fucker try to drown ya in the name of his imaginary sky fairy. You might not recall, but I do. You were fuckin' terrified and traumatised. You screamed the fuckin' place down and for the next year afterwards, bath time was a nightmarish reliving of that fateful day. You do remember the years that followed though. Earliest memories of Sunday mornings, goin' with Mum 'n' Dad back to that shithole to have the fear of god hammered into ya with nine inch nails of bullshit.

It's not even 4AM and Father *Fiddler* will still be asleep in his quarters. Make a quick stop home first. I have plans which will require the use of your Bowie knife. That's right, mate; you're about to break another egg. Might not use this one for your omelette though; this egg is rotten as fuck.

The streets are still empty, so why are ya doin' the speed limit? Man, you have some serious unlearnin' to do. Fuckin' step on it!

***

Holy Trinity Catholic Church: Would ya look at this joint! What a pretentious, elaborately designed monstrosity, and these cunts preach humility and frugality. Check out the BMW – wait, fuck, he has two!

All these shit-brained social commentators

loudly blaming the lower class no-hopers on welfare for bein' a burden on the economy. Here's the real burden. This is where a lot of your hard stolen tax dollars go, while these cunts don't pay a single fucking cent to live in luxury and convince their idiot flock of sheep to give 'em even more money. Fuckin' parasites.

You can take care of his sweet rides after. Ya don't wanna alert him to your presence until you're hoverin' over his bed, blade in hand. Grab the crowbar, you'll need it to jimmy open his door.

***

Sleepin' like a baby. Look at the fat fuck. I bet he eats well every night. Give him a nice whack on the head with the crowbar, but don't kill him – not just yet.

Holy shit! Fucking disgraceful piece of human garbage! Is that a boy beside him? Man, I shouldn't be surprised, but this complicates matters somewhat. Even I feel bad about this, but you're gonna hafta take care of him. Tie the lad up, gag him and lock him in that closet. He doesn't need to see what's about to go down. Be careful not to hurt him, remember…don't be a cunt. Poor kid. He probably has no idea that what he's been havin' done to him is despicable and wrong.

I know, you just wanna bash this fucker's brains to mush, but he has to suffer first. This is the lowest act of depravity I can think of, and people have no fucking idea what goes on in the privacy of his bed. I am almost inclined to stand back and watch you go to town on him, but let's be methodical about this, yeah?

Cut the cunt's tongue out first. Ya don't want his screams to traumatise the kid more than he already is. Just rip it out of his mouth and slice – don't be gentle. This should rouse him from the light clobberin' ya just gave him.

Brilliant, he's awake haha! Oh, that terror in his eyes is just divine, yeah? Drag him out onto the floor and grab that nice, thick candle. Aw, how helpful he is. He's already naked. Piece of shit. Make him kneel, good, now shove his face into the floor and shove that candle deep into his filthy arse. *Use the force, Luke*; he's got room in there.

I see you are enjoying yourself again. You're a sadistic fuck, aren't ya? Layin' the boot in to kick that candle up into his guts is a particularly savage touch haha. Gotta say, I'm enjoying the show myself. He's gettin' what he deserves.

Boot him onto his back. There's one more thing you need to do to finish him off. That's the way. Now cut his fuckin' cock off. He won't be puttin' that where it don't belong anymore. A tongueless scream is a scream nonetheless. You've made some room in that filthy mouth of his, now stuff it with a dick fatter than he's used to takin' in his gob.

Nicely done, mate. Now burn this fuckin' house of depravity and lies to the ground and let's get the hell outta here. Grab the kid first and take him to the carpark. He won't go anywhere bound like that.

A glorious sight, innit? A holy funeral pyre for a disgustingly unholy cunt. Good riddance, Father Fiddler. May you rot in your imaginary Hell.

***

Ok, what's next? You're gettin' the hang of this; time for you to think for yourself again. It'll be daylight soon, so where do ya wanna go now? What's another institution designed to enslave? Yes, you've got it. School.

Thirteen years of indoctrination into a system where you are taught, above any academic learning, to be obedient and follow an insane number of ludicrous rules. They want you just smart enough to be a productive worker and just stupid enough to swallow the bullshit they force down your throats without ever questioning their authority.

In many ways, the education system is far more insidious than organised religion.

You seem to have developed a pattern here. I think arson at the local public school is in order. Burn it to ashes before the day of indoctrination begins for hundreds of slaves in the makin'. Should be easy enough. Just head straight for the office, break in and light that fucker up; the rest should take care of itself.

***

Good on ya, mate, you're learnin'. I didn't need to remind ya of the 'road rules' haha. Pull right up to the office. Dawn is fast approachin' and ya want a clean, quick getaway before the world wakes up to another day of slavery. Ok, let's do this. Don't forget ya trusty crowbar.

Now, you're gonna have to be quick. You'll have less than a minute to get in there, trash the joint, and light the fucker up before the alarm sounds. This one will be risky, but you've got this. Just smash the glass outta the door, get in and get out.

Fuck! The alarm was instant! Quick, do what ya came to do and let's get the fuck outta here. Plenty of paper in this office to start a nice bonfire, now light it up!

Your efficiency is impressive haha, now let's get outta here before the pigs arrive. Shit. Sirens. They're onto ya, man, now double time, back to the car – LET'S GO!

They're here! They've blocked ya in. Only way out is through; there's only one option. Fuckin' ram the cunts.

BLAM! BLAM! BLAM!

Keep goin'! Get the fuck away, mate! Oh shit, you're hit. Watch out for that pole! FUUUUUUCK!

Sorry, man. Maybe we were a little hasty with

this last venture. I know it hurts. Can you still hear me? Look, you made only a small dent in your journey to freedom, but it was a significant shift in your awakening before 'The Man' came 'n took it all away. Just keep this in mind as you fade away. You may be dying, but you are leaving this world…

A FREE MAN.

Q: What's one thing you NEVER call a crazy person?

A: Crazy.

The world is full of crazies: sociopaths, psychopaths, these 'paths' and those 'paths'; a cornucopia of different disorders and derangements. We have 'em all, and while our many institutions overflow with such colourful folk, they also walk en masse amongst us. Be careful who you let into your home and into your lives. Beware those petty pleasantries and always look behind the 'mask of socialisation'.

This first appeared in the Project 26 anthology, PSYCHO PATH by J. Ellington Ashton Press.

https://www.amazon.com/Psycho-Path-Project-26-Book-ebook/dp/B0755DW7DM/

Petty Pleasantries

Yeah, y'know what? She was right. I *am* wrong. Now, don't get me wrong. I was right. I mean, I'm *always* right. I know my damn job better than anyone else in the business, but man, am I just *wrong*! I don't need you to tell me that though, and I damn well didn't need her tellin' me that either. She was very *wrong* to do so. The last thing I need is some skanky housewife bitch tellin' me I'm wrong. That's the last thing I need *anyone* tellin' me! Screw them! – right in the neck – with a flathead screwdriver! So yeah, that's just what I did. Like I said… *wrong*.

So now I have a dead body on my hands – another one; bloody hell, and it looks like it's about to become two. It couldn't have happened at a more inopportune moment, but this one asked for it. They all ask for it. Do you have any idea how insulting it is to be told you're just not right in the head? All I'm tryin' to do is help people and this is the kind of thanks I get? Geez, the nerve of some people.

They always seem nice enough to start with,

y'know, when I first turn up on their doorstep, toolbox in hand, and we exchange those initial, essential pleasantries. It's all part of the job and I don't really care how their day might be goin'. Hell, I know they don't really care how my day is goin' – just empty, petty pleasantries to get me in the door and to wherever the problem is that needs fixin'.

I'm a handyman. I'm my own boss, have my own little business and I do pretty well for myself. Luckily, I don't work for a company, or let's face it, I'd be screwed. Hehe... get it? Screwed? Never mind. That's just a little joke hehe. But in all seriousness, I am good at what I do.

You couldn't exactly say I come highly recommended. More often than not, my customers don't live long enough to recommend my services to anyone. I was just clever enough to name my company 'AAA Fix It' and claim my spot at the top of the phone directory listing for home repair services, so yeah, I get a lot of work.

Sure, there's a few of 'em who are just a downright pleasure to be of service to, but most of 'em can be bloody rude, and a little presumptuous and demanding even. Then ya get those right stuck up folk who think just because I have come to do their menial dirty work, I am somehow below 'em – a lowly scumbag labourer. I'll have you know, there ain't a problem I can't fix, except one I s'pose, but that's not part of the job description. My problem is my temper, and that often gets me into sticky predicaments like the one I'm in now.

So, I get the call to come out and fix a blocked kitchen sink. Simple, quick fix which'll make me a nice, tidy sum. I'm not dumb. I quote for my services at a rate depending on the area, and this call came from the ritzy part of town. I know I could have even thrown an extra fifty bucks on top of my quote with this job, but I'm not a greedy man. I could tell by the voice on the phone, that she would've had no problem agreeing to whatever ridiculous price I quoted her. She sounded pretty high strung and desperate to have her problem resolved ASAP.

I pull into her drive and get out of my old workhorse van. I need a new vehicle. This one has seen better days, I tell ya. It looks real outta place, parked here; nice, perfectly manicured lawns on a sprawling property, the driveway itself, over two hundred metres long from road to door, curling and weaving around stone statue ornaments and an obscenely large water feature. Completely asinine and not practical at all. Why not just have a bloody driveway that leads straight from the road to the house? I was gettin' pissed off just tryin' to navigate my way around these pretentious additions without clippin' one on the way past. Not off to a good start, lady. Not off to a good start at all.

This house is bloody huge! Three storey, gaudy lookin' mansion type joint. It's got an oversized marble staircase leading to the front door; equally oversized with stained glass panelling and a giant, ornate round doorknob. I was thinkin', '*I hate this bitch already.*' I was tempted to smack my old metal toolbox against the steps on the way up and take out a chip or two, but I refrained. For all I know, she's at the door now, watchin' me approach through those stained door panels.

By the time I got from my van to the front door, I had already started to work up a sweat. My mood was already beginning to teeter on the edge.

One of those stupid turnkey doorbell things – you gotta be kiddin' me. I knocked…hard and several times.

Sure enough, before I finish my knuckle assault on the solid oak door, it opens and there stands a classy lookin' broad, even though she's barefoot 'n' wearin' nothin' more than a red and gold silk kimono. I guess it was the way she held herself; confident, sultry – seductive even. She looked to be in her early forties and was quite the babe. The way she stood there, blockin' the way and lookin' at me like she wanted to jump my bones; not sayin' a word, like she was waitin' for me to introduce myself before she was gonna let me in.

"AAA Fix It, love. I'm here to fix your kitchen sink."

"Sure," she says. "Please, come in. My name is Mara."

"Todd. Thanks, love. So, where's this kitchen of yours?"

Now, to say this lady kept a clean joint would be an understatement. The place was spotless, immaculate. She stood aside and let me in, then closed the door behind us.

"Could you leave your shoes at the door here, please?"

"Um, no. Sorry, love. Don't want me droppin' a tool on my foot or somethin' like that, y'know? Safety regulations 'n' all that. I wouldn't wanna have to hit ya up for compensation if I were to injure myself now, would I?" She didn't like that much at all. Her eyes narrowed and her face screwed up in an indignant pout. You could tell she wasn't used to bein' told 'No'.

"Very well. Follow me please," she says then turns kinda over-dramatically and starts leadin' me into her *humble* abode.

What an arse! This bitch is hot, and she knows it. Her slow, sexy strut has all the hallmarks of a bored, lonely housewife. Hubby away on business and she wants a little bit of action while he's gone. I know the type, but I'm not that type. I'm here to do a job, get paid and get the hell out. Still, doesn't hurt to cop an eyeful every now 'n' then, y'know?

So, you remember me remarking on the spotlessness of this joint, right? Well, that's where things turned ugly. We walk into the kitchen and I get straight to work. Place my toolbox on the kitchen bench and pull open the cupboard doors beneath the sink.

"Excuse me, could you please not leave that filthy thing on the bench?"

Here we go... "Sorry, love." I take it down and plonk it on the tiled floor with a loud *clank*.

"Be careful!"

Bloody hell woman. Don't you start! I could feel that hotness in my cheeks, the tightness in my chest, that vein throbbin' in my temple; tappin' out a Morse code SOS to that part of my brain that wants so badly to react. I stay crouched, pretending to look under the sink but really, I am just doin' everything in my power to calm the hell down.

A single bead of sweat forms on my brow and trickles down into my eye, the salty sting causin' it to twitch in a disjointed dance with the throbbin' temple vein. Deep breaths, Todd... Deeeep breaths.

"Sorry, love."

"Please stop calling me *love*. I told you, my name is Mara."

Fuck… "Sorry – *Mara*."

This bitch is gonna make me snap, I just know it.

So, I'm fiddlin' around with the pipe, pretending to inspect where the problem is, when in reality, I'm just waitin' for her to stop hoverin' around me like a persistent fart 'n' let me get on with my job.

"Listen, love – *Mara*. Can ya leave me to it and before ya know it, I'll be all done 'n' outta your hair? Cheers love, I mean, *Mara*. Sorry."

"Fine. Just don't make a mess of the place."

I didn't reply. Kept my mouth shut because I knew the next thing to come outta my mouth wasn't gonna be pretty. I watched from the corner of my eye as she spun once again in an unnecessarily dramatic fashion and pranced out of the room; that cute little arse of hers flickin' side to side as she went. *Slut.*

Finally left alone, I began to get down to business. I opened my tool box and started pullin' stuff out and spreadin' it out on the floor beside me to get to the tools I needed. This wasn't gonna take long and for that, I was glad. The longer I stayed in this sterile joint, the more my temper began to rise. I took my wrench and laid it in front of me, then reached for the screwdriver.

"What the hell are you doing? Didn't I specifically say not to make a mess? Are you freakin' insane?!"

Insane? INSANE? Biiig mistake lady. You can call me anything, but you DON'T call me insane, mad, nuts, what the hell ever! That shit is just not on.

She was standin' right over me like some silky red bloody hovercraft or some crap like that, so I stabbed my screwdriver straight through her bare foot. She screamed and pulled her foot away, the screwdriver still firm in my grip. She lost her balance, slippin' in the sudden pool of blood, and hit the tiles hard.

Insane, am I?

She was wailin' like a damn banshee and my blood was boilin'. I needed to shut this bitch up before the whole neighbourhood came a runnin'. I grabbed her leg and half dragged her to me, half dragged myself up and on top of her. At this point, you do understand, I was in no rational frame of mind. All I wanted was for the screamin' to stop, so then began the frenzied screwdriver attack; stabbin' frantically into her throat until the screams turned into chokin' gurgles and then, the oh so sweet silence.

As I sat there, the rage subsiding, my serenity was shattered by a boisterous poundin' on the front door.

"Hello? Mara? Is everything OK in there?"

Dammit! What now? I got up off the floor, blood all over me, and started pacin' the kitchen while the knockin' persisted and my vision began turnin' back to red.

"Mara? Are you OK? Who's in there with you?"

"It's OK, love!" I called out. "Just the handy man. I'm here fixin' the sink!"

"Where's Mara? I heard a scream! Mara? Mara! Open this door instantly!"

Well, shit. This old biddy is makin' more racket out there than Mara did in here.

"Comin', love!" I called back, picked up my trusty wrench and went to let ol' sticky beak bossy boots in. I stopped at the door, shakin' with adrenaline and tryin' to breathe.

"Open this door!" So I did. I must've looked a real sight, sweatin' like an athlete 'n' splattered in blood.

"What th…" The ol' bat from next door didn't get to finish her exclamation. I grabbed her by the hair and quickly pulled her inside the door, kickin' it shut and smashin' the wrench hard over her head. Well damn, that was easy. Killed her in one blow. I left her there, twitchin' in the foyer and returned to the kitchen, and yes, I fixed the damn sink. I am a professional, after all.

After the job was done – and a good job it was, if I do say so myself – I packed up my tools and went to the bathroom to clean myself up. Once I'd cleaned off the blood as best I could, I went searchin' for that Mara bitch's purse. I wasn't leavin' here without gettin' paid. Not after all the extra work I'd put in. I found it in her bedroom, and why the hell not? I took that extra fifty bucks I'd initially considered quotin' for the job. Money well earned for havin' to put up with such a rude customer, I reckon.

I grabbed my toolbox and left, steppin' over

the old lady corpse in the foyer on my way out, and got to my van quick smart. As soon as I sat down behind the wheel, my phone rang.

"G'day, AAA Fix It. How can I help ya? ..... Faulty wiring? Sure, I can fix that no problems. Just finished up at a job, so I'll be right over. What's your address, love?"

WHAT'S IN A NAME? is a horrific story of torture, played out by a distraught father and a sick, disgusting paedophile. This tale is a brutal account of one man's mental anguish and subsequent revenge, and another 'poor excuse for a' man's agonising end.

Eye have to add here; this story fukks with me. It is by far my most disturbing and horrific tale, and it is quite likely to leave a nasty taste in your mouth upon finishing it. Fair warning.

Appearing in REJECTED For Content 3, of the extreme anthology series by J. Ellington Ashton Press.

https://www.amazon.com/Rejected-Content-3-Vicious-Vengeance-ebook/dp/B016RH95OG/

What's in a Name?

"All you have to do is say his name. Just speak his name and He will come. Then, fiend... It will finally be over".

"Rishhh...Rshh". The blind man lay naked, prone and broken across the large wheel, positioned horizontally face down and bound with all manner of restraints. His broken left hand, manacled in a rusted iron fetter, dangled limply over the rim. The right; equally mangled, held fast with dirty copper wire. His fingers, swollen and purple from deprivation of blood flow, had stiffened and now stretched helplessly toward some invisible salvation, as he unsuccessfully tried to give his torturer what he demanded.

The fact he was barely conscious, making it a struggle to form a coherent word, was compounded by the seven fish hooks attached to the wheel by short lengths of twine and roughly pierced through his lower lip. Countless times as he would begin to fade, his tormentor had pulled his head up by the fringe, 'accidentally' tearing a hook or two free. Soon, there would be no more lip to re-hook.

"His name," the obese and foul reeking Merwin repeated patiently; this time, more tenderly lifting the head and bringing a flask to the dying man's mouth. As he tipped it up to pour the liquid, his victim gagged and spluttered as the burning taste of Merwin's disgusting piss spilled onto his tongue, immediately running back out over his hanging, disfigured lip.

Merwin was taking great delight in this wretch's suffering. He had spent months planning for this precious time with his captive. This deplorable creature who had left him without family. Who had walked free from the courts and from custody, acquitted of any charge.

This thing no longer had the dignity of a name. The man who lay bound and broken before him had once been a close and trusted friend to Merwin, his late wife and four year old son. That trust had been insidiously betrayed time and time again as Merwin and his dearly departed Marie lived the high life; frequenting parties where they would rub shoulders with the society elite, whilst their young boy was left at home in the sordid care of this filth.

"His   NAME!"   Merwin   screamed.   He slammed his flask down on top of the bastard's head, driving his face into the wheel. Hooks tore through mashed gum flesh, already beginning to turn septic, and the sting of metal, faeces and urine drew a feeble attempt at a wail from the man's swollen throat.

Merwin hoped with all his being that this pathetic creature would continue to hang in there. He had to control his rage and the near insurmountable urge to simply beat him to bloody death. His prisoner's suffering was paramount to Merwin and he would draw it out for as long as he could contain himself.

Bent, rusted nails still protruded through the lids from each sightless eyeball. Those eyes had rested upon his dear boy too many times for Merwin to abide. They were among the first anatomy of this wretch to be disabled.

Trembling with the wrath that churned his insides, Merwin walked around the wheel to his victim's feet. Picking up the mallet and a six inch concreting nail from the nearby bench, he turned back to his prey. Positioning the nail beside several more just above the ankle, he drove the mallet down hard. The nail penetrated the flesh and passed instantly through the already disintegrated bone, disappearing into the wheel rim.

The man screamed and his body convulsed. The barbed wire wrapped up and down his body, holding him fast to the spokes, tore and wriggled deeper into his back, and a sizable piece of lip detached and fell, swinging on the end of the disengaged fish hook.

"Rrriii-ih-ih-ih!" The broken man sobbed in hopeless agony as he desperately tried to speak his name. The child he had violated. The boy who he had subjected to humiliation and agony; at his own hands and those of the inhuman filth who visited while Merwin and Marie socialised, oblivious to the horrors that transpired in their home.

Merwin shuddered at the sound of the man's scream and heard the voice of his own son, imagining with impotent rage, his terrified, anguished cries and pleas. What inhuman monsters could be so callous with a child of such tender age?

Then his thoughts turned to Marie. His devastated wife. Once they had learned of the atrocities performed on their son in the perceived safety of their home, with the man they had entrusted with his care, Marie had drowned the poor boy in the bath before dragging a razor across her jugular, and bleeding out swiftly into the tub.

"Give me his fucking naaame! Give! Me! His! Name!" He emphasised each word with a savage stab into the back of the scum's thigh with a large screwdriver, ending his final word with a cruel twist that tore the flesh, the muscle and gouged at bone with a squishing, grating sound. This time, no scream escaped the man's throat. The desecrated body just twitched and shivered in mild convulsion. He had again fallen unconscious.

Merwin took shaky steps backwards and rested against his table of implements. He had to be careful. He had been at it for hours now. So many times he'd had to stop himself from taking it to an untimely end. His prisoner had lost copious amounts of blood and had passed out from the severe torture numerous times. If Merwin wasn't vigilant, he would lose the wretch before he got the desired response.

Cries and screams were secondary to Merwin. He wanted the name. He needed to hear his son's name pass from the lips of this despicable piece of worm shit.

Dejectedly, he pushed himself from the table and went for the hose. This fucker wasn't going to die on him just yet. Pointing the nozzle at the lifeless lump's face, he turned the tap to full blast. What remained of his victim's lip fell away on the ends of the hooks, as his head reacted violently to the drowning deluge of water shocking him back into consciousness. Merwin turned the hose away and shut off the water.

He looked at the pathetic creature before him with malice as the broken man spluttered and howled in unspeakable agony. The screwdriver still lodged in his leg and the barbs dug deep into the mutilated flesh of his back; inwardly, he prayed for Death.

* * *

'Had it been worth it?' he mused through the haze of his delirium. The 'private' parties he had

hosted at the abode of his old friend whilst they were away, catered to some of the wealthiest and most publicly well respected vermin from the highest echelons of a morally depraved society.

A conspiracy of paedophilia, ritual sacrifice and murder ran rife through their ranks, and reached its evil fingers into nearly all aspects of the social order. Touching in every corner of the globe, the organisation included everyone from presidents to priests; from magistrates to hospital matrons. To protect their secrecy and keep their anonymity, he was never going to be held accountable for his crimes... or so he had thought.

Merwin and Marie had begun to suspect something was not right, as their son developed bizarre behavioural changes. Nightmares, bedwetting, bouts of screaming and a look of terror in the poor child's face when left alone for no longer than a minute. He would always refuse to talk about it when confronted. Instead, the boy would become hysterical and violent.

When the horrifying truth began to come to light through psychologist and hospital visits, this scum became suddenly scarce, and the distraught parents knew instantly that he was the cause of their child's torment.

He was subsequently found and arrested, was stood to trial and unbelievably, after all the evidence of his debauchery had been presented, walked away free. His ill-gained freedom lasted seven months. Only through the desolation and devastation of Merwin, who had gone into recluse, was he afforded such an extended liberty. With his beloved family taken from him, Merwin kept to his home for several months and let himself wallow in his insurmountable grief. When the grief eventually turned to emptiness, the void began to fill with thoughts of revenge.

* * *

Merwin's basement provided him with the perfect torture chamber. He had begun to collect tools and various household items from around his home, to be assembled in his subterranean room of terror. He had spent the better part of a month building his sadistic wheel of torture, all the while fantasising about how it would be put to use. Once set up, his reflections turned to the scum who he would be accommodating in his torture chamber. Merwin sat in the basement, trying to recall all the favourite haunts of the man he would soon kill slowly. He had all but vanished after the court hearings and Merwin hoped he had not fled the area entirely.

The following weeks would be spent driving around the sleepy town where he resided. Bars, cafes, even the local library he knew this bastard would frequent, but to no avail. He had indeed seemed to have skipped town. Merwin refused to accept that his quarry was altogether gone, however. He would find him, and he would make him know the true meaning of suffering and agony.

He expanded his perimeter to the adjoining towns, determined to hunt him down. After another week of searching, Merwin's efforts were finally rewarded. He recognised the car; a silver BMW with dark tinted windows and personalized number plates that read, 'BILL.ME'. A foolish choice of transport for one who was apparently trying to remain inconspicuous, were the immediate musings that crossed Merwin's mind.

The hour was late. Nearing eleven pm. Merwin drove around the corner, locked his car and made his way back to the BMW. At the rear passenger door, he produced a claw hammer and was about to smash the window, before thinking to check if the car was locked. It wasn't. He opened the door, then climbed into the back to wait.

Merwin wasn't waiting long when his target returned to the car. Upon entering and inserting his key, he was surprised by his old friend appearing in the rear vision mirror. Merwin gave him a half-hearted whack in the side of the head with his hammer.

"Drive, or the next one will spill your brains across this nice leather upholstery. We're going home, you piece of shit." Merwin didn't say another word apart from "drive" or "my house," when asked their intended destination, for the half hour journey back to his place. He just gazed at the back of this wretch's skull, ignoring the pleas for reason emanating from the front.

As they pulled into the drive, Merwin raised the automatic garage door, and the BMW rolled inside to a halt. As soon as the engine ceased, Merwin gave the man three quick and savage blows to the head with his hammer, then alighted from the car on the driver's side. He opened the door and dragged the stunned bastard out by his hair, hitting him haphazardly with the hammer as he did so.

Throwing him to the ground, the image of his child danced vividly in his mind's eye, and Merwin broke into a rage of solid kicks into the exposed ribs of this disgusting paedophile, coupled with a pouring of hammer blows to wherever they may land. Before long, the agonised cries for mercy stopped, as did his attempts to cover up from the vicious attack. He was unconscious and would not re-awaken until he was bound tightly and cruelly to the wheel in Merwin's basement.

His feet tied together firmly with a length of rope, he was dragged through the garage door into the adjoining house. Merwin felt an exhilaration course through his body at the thought of what lay ahead. At the top of the basement stairs, he paused for a moment. He was ready to just toss this garbage down them into the basement, but stopped himself. The fall may kill the bastard, and thus put an impromptu end to his sadistic plans. Instead, Merwin lifted the unconscious man under the armpits and dragged him down the steep staircase, into the dimly lit room below.

Before he could begin with the retribution however, Merwin would have to take the car back to where he had found it and retrieve his own vehicle. There was still abundant time before daybreak, and he was very keen to get started... but first things first.

Grabbing another length of rope, Merwin proceeded to bind the hands tightly behind and wrap the remainder of rope around the inert body, securing it to the leg of his solid worktable. He then carefully placed some heavy shelving across the man, who lay face down on the stone floor, to prevent him from moving around and possibly escaping his bonds, tight as they were.

Satisfied with his efforts, Merwin left him and returned to the BMW. He wanted to get this menial task out of the way as swiftly as possible, but maintained his composure so as not to arouse any attention. He slowly backed out of the garage, and left for the neighbouring town.

* * *

As he drove, Merwin reminisced of the times he and Marie had attended these high class dinners and parties. The food and alcoholic refreshments at these soirées had been impeccable. The hosts and other guests, questionable but pleasant enough. Merwin and his wife had considered themselves very fortunate and honoured to be invited and included in these gatherings.

At this moment, however, it began to dawn on Merwin that perhaps they had been invited merely as a ruse. A subterfuge that enabled their so-called 'friend' to use their home – and their only child – in degenerate parties of an entirely different nature.

There had been evidence of activity from several people in their home while they were out, but they had overlooked it and put it down to their 'friend' simply making himself at home. That was fine. They had insistently assured him to do so, as he was doing them a great favour in taking care of their son.

Who were these people? These scum of the earth, who had set Merwin and Marie up in this elaborate deception? He noticed he had begun to press his foot down on the pedal as he fumed.

"Slow down, Merwin," he told himself aloud. "Let's not get caught, ok?"

He arrived at his destination quicker than he had expected, much to his morbid delight. He stepped out of the car, leaving it unlocked as he had found it, and returned to his own around the corner. As he fired up the engine, Merwin was brought back to his original resolve and without wasting another moment, sped off back home.

His thoughts meandered as he drove, between the events that had led him to this moment and the events that this moment was to lead him towards. He once again began to wonder, who else would frequent these gatherings in his home while he and Marie were absent.

The parasite in his basement used to be a mortgage broker with one of the big banks before the trial. He had connections with the rich and powerful across the country and indeed, the world. Quite often,

Merwin had felt out of place at the parties he and his wife would attend. He felt like they were a part of some sort of charade. The people in attendance had a forced, somewhat artificial air about them. Merwin's blood began to boil at the thought of being duped so thoroughly.

He was only around the corner from home and he had many questions for his prisoner. He wanted names. Every name this piece of shit associated with. Above all, he wanted him to speak one name in particular. His son. His treasured little boy who these bastards had terrorised and treated like a faceless, nameless object. Pulling into his garage and the roller door closing behind him, Merwin was more than eager to get to work.

Upon entering the basement, he was pleased to see his prisoner still unconscious and bound, just as he had left him. Lifting the shelving from the man, a short gasp escaped his lungs from the release of pressure, but he did not stir.

Merwin stood over the man and lifted him under the arms to the wheel, placing him face down across it. Removing the rope and the bastard's shirt, he positioned him on the wheel. Securing the left hand tightly in the manacle, he stretched the right arm across and proceeded to wrap the other hand mercilessly with the attached wire. Before securing the feet with more copper wire, Merwin removed the man's shoes and pants.

Once bound with no hope of escape, Merwin set about reviving the scum so the real business could get underway.

"Wake up!" Merwin yelled into the man's face as he held his head up by the hair. "Wake up!" he repeated with two sharp slaps. His eyes opened to see the determined scowl on Merwin's face dominating his vision. Fear began to spread across his visage as he became aware of his predicament, and for the briefest moment, Merwin balked.

"You are not human," he said in disgust. More to reassure himself than anything. The atrocity strapped to his wheel shivered and winced in pain as he tried to hold Merwin's gaze. He knew it was all over. There was nothing he could possibly say to the vengeful father that would release him from this retribution. Without a word, he lowered his face in shame.

"We are going to systematically address my concerns, regarding your involvement with my dear son, may he rest in peace," Merwin began. The man groaned and kept his gaze to the floor beneath him.

"Look at me!" Merwin howled at him and the man raised his head, unsteadily. Shocking pain shot through his skull and limbs from the hammer blows he had already endured, but this had been nothing more than the precursor to the agonised end of his life. Tears welled in Merwin's eyes and began to fall.

"I trusted you. *We* trusted you! What kind of creature are you? He was four years old, you bastard. Four fucking years old!" The hammer still in his hand, Merwin brought it down onto the left wrist with a sick thud. Bones split and crumbled and an inhuman wail of torment sounded throughout the chamber. It had begun.

"Please," the desperate man begged, "Please stop. I'll do whatever you want. Please, just stop."

"I imagine you're using the very words my son used when pleading for mercy. I should rip that filthy tongue right out of your head, but you are going to talk first. Who else did you have in my house while my wife and I were away? Who else had their disgusting way with my little boy?" No response resulted in another hammer strike on the same, destroyed hand and the howling scream that ensued turned Merwin's blood to ice.

"You will talk. You will tell me everything and maybe, you will be spared an agonising death. Remain silent, and silence will be your eternal companion. Now, who else was in my house?"

"I don't know who they were. Everybody would arrive wearing a mask. Anonymity was a prerequisite. Please, Merwin. I beg you, please, let me go."

"If I were to show you pictures, could you identify them?" Merwin asked the baiting question.

"No, I couldn't. They were always in disguise."

"I see," Merwin replied. He dropped the hammer to the floor, which gave his prisoner a jump, then walked around behind him to his table.

"What are you doing?" the man cried desperately, but Merwin said nothing. He returned to the head of the wheel and squatted down before his prey. The nails in his hand were rusted and crooked, but he had prepared them specially, weeks before. Sharpening their points with a grinder until they were needle thin and keeping them in a container of his son's grave dirt, he had plans for these two nails. He grabbed the man by his ear and pressed his thumb down over his eyelid.

"Your eyes will serve you no purpose, then." He slowly poked the tip of the nail through the eyelid and the man began to thrash about wildly, screaming in terror. Merwin was unable to push the nail through with his prisoner carrying on like this. He was planning to save this for later but…what the hell. He dropped the nails on the floor and grabbed him by his fringe. With three solid face slams into the wheel, the man became still and silent.

Now, Merwin went to work with the fish hooks. No sooner had he fed the first hook through the flesh of this parasite's lower lip, he awoke with another scream and more wild thrashing. Merwin held his head still as, one by one, he roughly pierced the hooks all along the lip. Maybe now, he wouldn't be so keen to throw his head around.

"Let's try that again," Merwin announced and retrieved the nails from the floor. Once more, he took the man's ear, pressed his eye shut, and pushed the nail straight through the eyelid and into the eye.

"These eyes have seen more of my son than I can bear to imagine. They will see no more." Merwin's voice was drowned out by the anguished screams as his prisoner's eye popped and squelched at the intrusion. In his struggle, all that was achieved was a fish hook ripping through his lip, to hang swinging below his face. The other six remained painfully intact. Merwin pushed the man's face into the hard wooden rim of the wheel.

"One down, one to go. But first, let me fix this for you." Holding his head still, he re-attached the fish hook and brought his face up until his lower lip was pulled taut. Pressing the other lid down with his thumb, Merwin repeated the process with a bit more ease. The searing pain was too much for the maggot and he passed out cold on the wheel.

Merwin felt mildly satisfied with the proceedings thus far, and relished the momentary peace and quiet, whilst contemplating the next step. He was far too unrestrained for Merwin's liking, so he fetched a long length of barbed wire from the far corner of the room. Wearing a pair of welding gloves, he attached the wire fast to the wheel and pulled it across the man's shoulders, reached beneath him and yanked it tight around him. Again, the screams began.

Partially ignoring and at the same time, greatly enjoying the terrible sounds of suffering, Merwin continued to wrap the barbed wire around the entire torso, giving a solid tug at each round. The barbs dug into and tore at the flesh of his back and sides.

"Who is behind all of this?" Merwin asked. "These parties that Marie and I attended... Were they involved?"

"Yes... Yes. I don't know who the organiser is. Nobody does. It's a vast network that spreads all around the globe." Speaking was indeed difficult with seven pieces of metal securing his face to the wheel, but he was determined to tell Merwin what he knew, which wasn't very much. The secrecy of this demented society was of the utmost importance. In instances such as the one he had now found himself, secrecy was an obvious necessity. "If you let me live, I can take you to where they meet."

"How about you just tell me," Merwin replied. He wasn't buying this. Not for a second.

"I don't know," the pathetic worm broke into sobs. "All I know is it's a warehouse a few streets away from the docks. I couldn't tell you the address."

"I think I have just the thing to refresh your memory," Merwin said. As he walked around the wheel, the man lay still, trying to hear what his captor was doing. He felt a cold tickle on his left ankle as Merwin placed the nail. The next moment was filled with blinding agony. The nail pierced straight through his ankle and into the wood with the first hit. Two more strikes for good measure pushed it the rest of the way through. Once again, he fell unconscious.

A horrid stench began to make itself apparent. The bastard had shit himself and pissed himself all at once. Unpleasant, but Merwin didn't allow the reek to ruffle him. Instead, he used the glove to collect a small specimen, returned to the head of the wheel and wiped the excrement roughly over the man's savaged lip.

"Wake up!" Merwin bellowed and rapped his knuckles soundly atop the man's skull. He roused suddenly and pulled his head back, tearing two hooks through his shit smeared lip.

"Now, we're going to do this again... and again, and again, until you give me what I want," said Merwin as he found some un-torn lip to re-hook. He sounded almost playful, but it was the voice of somebody nigh on losing his patience.

He picked up the claw hammer again and with no further warning, commenced a frenzied hammer attack on the as yet untouched right hand, until it was split, swollen and contorted, wrapped tightly in copper wire.

Once again, the screaming was intolerable. In his struggle to escape the onslaught, he had torn all but two hooks from his degraded mouth, and now struggled to remain as still as possible. Merwin had stopped mere seconds after he began, but for his victim, it seemed to have gone on for minutes.

"So, you can't tell me who is involved in this sick little circle of yours? That's ok. I will find that out on my own." Merwin squatted in front of the broken man, the hammer held dangling between his legs. "I have your wallet. I have your phone, your house keys. I will find out what I want to know before anyone even realises you're gone."

Merwin pressed the hammer on the forehead of his prisoner and pushed his head up to meet his glare with nailed shut eyes. In a quiet voice, trembling with unmitigated contempt, each word delivered like a hammer blow.

"There is one name I know you can give me. Did they know my son's name? Or was he just a nameless plaything? I want to hear you say his name, you fucking parasite. Tell me my son had a name!"

His demand was again answered with a shame filled, downward blind stare. His raspy breath, and the rising and falling of dribbling whimpers and moans, grated on Merwin's nerves. It was one thing to take out his rage on the man who had committed the ultimate betrayal of trust, but just being in the presence of this oxygen thief filled Merwin with such disgust. Every moment was a tax on his patience, and that time was imminent where patience would no longer exist.

With a sigh, Merwin stood up and quietly walked around back. Moments later, a concreting nail was driven through the flesh, muscle and bone of the intact ankle. The ensuing scream was promptly cut short, as the man began vomiting fiercely and then passed out. Merwin continued to drive three more nails through the man's leg.

And here, Merwin stood. He had reached an impasse. He would have to find the names himself, and he was unsure whether his prisoner would even be capable of speaking his beloved son's name. The suffering and torture being inflicted was near inconsequential. Merwin had an overwhelming obsession to know that his child was not nameless throughout his ordeals. It seemed, the longer he kept this filth in his basement and the more Merwin dismantled him, the less likely he would get what he so desperately needed to hear.

The remainder of the session from this point on, had Merwin in a haze of dark and fleeting emotions. He would switch back and forth between in and out of control. Two more times, Merwin attacked the already destroyed hands. What those hands had done to his son boiled Merwin's blood. They had left their son in these, what they thought were *capable* hands. Merwin hated himself. How could he not have known...? That was enough musing. This bastard had had more than enough respite. It was time to hear his dear son's name.

He dropped the hammer at his feet. The man on the wheel didn't flinch. Merwin went back to his table of torment and picked up an old, rusted saw. He crouched down and reached beneath the wheel with his gloved hand, grabbing hold of the man's cock and balls in a maliciously firm grip. Shocked back into consciousness, the screaming began again in earnest.

"Shut Up!" Merwin shouted, with a harsh tug. As the screams faded to terrified moans of unspeakable pain, Merwin continued with a partial release of his cruel grip. "Tell me, fiend. What is my son's name?"

At this point, the damage done to the face and especially the mouth of this wretch had rendered him incapable of forming a word, no matter how hard he tried. He was so near to Death, and this was not going to stop for as long as he kept clinging to life. He was blearily unaware of what Merwin held in his other hand and was, at this point, beyond caring.

"Did you put this in my boy?" Merwin asked in a supressed rage, tightening his squeeze and pulling slowly downward. The broken man threw his head back, his lip already gone from his face, hanging in a display on seven separate hooks. A high pitched squeak followed by spastic gurgling was all that he was able to produce.

"His NAME!" Merwin screamed and began tearing through the base of the pervert's scrotum. It took him five swipes, back and forth, with the saw. On the severing swipe, he almost followed through to cut into his own arm, luckily managing to stop himself in time.

Blood pooled on the floor beneath the wheel in several spots. The gushing wound he had just inflicted made Merwin gag. He pulled himself to his feet, went back to the head of the wheel and stood there for a full minute, staring at his handiwork.

Merwin held his breath as he gazed intently over the inert form before him. The man was dead.

He had escaped Merwin's wrath, freed from the earthly responsibility to give a name to the human child he had used as an object. Merwin sat down heavily on the floor, knocking the wind out of himself in the process.

If there was a Hell, Merwin hoped what he had put that maggot through was just a brief taste of what was to come for him. As for Merwin, he didn't know what was real – Heaven. Hell. God. For all he knew, there was nothing. Nobody.

But maybe, just… maybe. Maybe it is true what they say. Our loved ones are waiting for us on the other side. There was nothing left for him here, so Merwin took his pistol from his coat pocket as he contemplated the unthinkable. Turning the piece over in his hands, making sure it was loaded… One in the chamber.

He sat for quite some time, recalling every moment he could, of his beloved wife and son. He called to them with his heart, cried out their names. They didn't answer his cries, or maybe Merwin just couldn't hear them.

"Marie, my dear Marie. Wait for me, please…!

Richard, my boy. My beautiful little Richard! Daddy's here! I won't let anything bad ever happen to you again!" He had the pistol pressed up under his chin and Merwin closed his eyes. Richard smiled his biggest, brightest beam and waved emphatically to his father.

Merwin pulled the trigger.

Never have been a fan of the 'Festive Season', or any of the Hallmark, 'consume, consume, consume' holiday dates spread strategically throughout the year for that matter. But Shitmas has to top my list of holiday hates.

But, when you are deep in the clutches of anthology addiction, and your publisher puts forward the idea of murdering your fellow authors and peers in a short story, well, concessions must inevitably be made.

Such was the case here. Eye was given the task of doing away with my good friend, Brian Barr (check him out on Amazon; he's ten hells of a killer author: https://www.amazon.com/Brian-Barr/e/B010Y0MEJU/) in which eye enjoyed – maybe just a lOttle bit too much – making his demise both, terrifying and humorous.

Appearing in the anthology SEASONS BLEEDINGS by J. Ellington Ashton Press, this was a surprisingly fun story for me to write and a rather fitting close to this little collection.

https://www.amazon.com/Seasons-Bleedings-Roma-Gray-ebook/dp/B01MPVOWZ4/

Sanity Korpse

It only happens once a year, but when you hear those slay bells a ringin', you might wanna find somewhere good to hide for the night. It's Stressmas time and y'know what that means, right? Yeah, that's right. Sanity Korpse is comin' to town. Hidin' isn't even a sure thing, but you at least gotta try if ya plan on seein' Boxing Day. He sees you when you're sleeping and, by jingles, he knows when you're awake! Doesn't really matter whether you've been bad or good, he'll rip out your entrails regardless, dangle ya over your open fireplace, and then light that fucker up with a demented "Ho Ho Ho".

They say that no good story starts with a glass of milk but let me tell you, my friends…this story does.

This year is Brian's fifth surviving Stressmas. Five years since Santa went insane and embarked on his first annual worldwide killin' spree—and it is all Brian's fault. Now, before we get down to the nitty gritty details of this year's festive season of slaughter, perhaps I should fill ya all in on what happened that fateful night, five years ago to the day.

Y'see, Brian was a stoner and a bit of a prankster too. He liked to get ripped off his nuts and play hilarious pranks on people. Well…hilarious to Brian at least. The recipients of his tomfoolery were rarely so amused, but at least Brian got a giggle out of it.

I remember this one time, when he was fresh out of college, he went down to the local supermarket with a Stanley knife and one of those tubes of fake vampire blood. He wandered down the breakfast aisle, slashin' and squirtin' his way through all the front rows of breakfast cereal boxes, leavin' a note – ransom style, with letters cut from news headlines in the paper – that simply read "CEREAL KILLER" stuck on the last remainin' box of Froot Loops.

He made the headlines in the local that week and was the top story on the six o'clock news that night. Funny fucker, although the store owner didn't see it that way. Cost the poor bastard hundreds of dollars in damaged stock, and Brian got away with it too. They never found out who the mysterious

"CEREAL KILLER" was. Anyway, we're gettin' a little off track here. Back to the story.

'Twas the night before Xmas, and Brian had scored himself a pound of the finest weed earlier that day. He'd got his work bonus before stoppin' for the break, so he decided to splash out and buy a hundred sheet of some pretty damn mind-blowin' acid as well.

So, there he was, trippin' off his guts and smokin' a big fat scoob in his favourite chair. He was admirin' his haphazard efforts of decoratin' his living room with coloured balls and long strands of tinsel, plus the tree he'd had an argument with that afternoon in old Mrs. Mavis's front yard.

He'd run home, screamin' blue murder back over his shoulder at the non-argumentative tree as he went, before returnin' with his trusty ol' axe to give it what for. Now it stood in the corner of the room, leanin' miserably against the wall.

While he sat there, the peak beginnin' to subside, Brian had a brilliant idea. He decided he was gonna prank none other than Santa himself! He reached into his bag and pulled out a huge handful of bud, took it with him to the kitchen, and got to work makin' a big batch of cookies. While they baked away in the oven, he poured a large glass of milk and dropped not one, not even ten, but no less than twenty-five tabs into it.

He let that sit on the counter and went back to his chair to stare at the tree some more. He was pretty sure it was dead, after bashing the shit out of it with his axe, but he just wanted to be sure it wasn't gonna try and get that last word in from the dispute in Mrs. Mavis's yard that day. The tree just stood there, lookin' defeated and finally, Brian tired of starin' it down. He was satisfied he'd won this fight.

Behind him, along the opposite wall, a large and well-stocked bar stood. Nobody but Brian was allowed behind it. He'd even made a big, colourful neon sign to hang above it that read 'BRIAN'S BAR'. His friends were most welcome to drink at Brian's Bar, as long as he was servin'.

That night, he was home alone and trippin' hard, so he decided to go play bartender to himself while he waited for the cookies to be done. All the while, twenty-five tabs of LSD leached their way into the glass of milk on the counter.

Finally, four double bourbons later, the oven timer went off, startlin' Brian right off his stool and onto his back on the floor. He jumped to his feet, fists up 'n' lookin' around wildly for the person who must've delivered that knockout blow and then doubled over in hysterics when he realised this was no boxing match. The cookies were ready!

He opened the oven and the heavenly aroma of dope scented chocolate wafted out, fillin' the room. Brian took a small saucer out of the cupboard and placed it next to the milk on the counter. Out of the twenty-four cookies, he took three and arranged them invitingly on the saucer.

He looked at the display, and then at his tray of twenty-one, stole some furtive glances all around the room before snatchin' one of the three from the saucer and stuffin' it in his gob. Takin' the tray of goodies back to his chair, he sat down to roll a big joint and giggle at his devious plan for the next three hours.

Brian's eyes watered profusely from his prolonged laughin' session, and he struggled to read the wavy hands of the clock on the wall. After several delirious minutes, he guessed at the time bein' a little bit past eleven. He gave one last warning glare at the dead tree in the corner, and got up from his chair to head off to bed. He didn't wanna be awake when Santa came down the chimney, although he would've given anything to see the look on his face when the milk 'n' cookies took effect.

He hadn't been in the land of nod for too long when Santa's sleigh landed silently on his roof, and the fat man in the red suit slipped down his chimney. Steppin' from the fireplace and brushin' himself off, Santa unhitched the sack from his shoulder and pulled out three brightly wrapped gifts. Takin' 'em over to the forlorn lookin' tree and placin' 'em at its base, he looked around for the customary snack, smilin' broadly when he saw the milk 'n' cookies sittin' innocently on the counter.

"Ooh! Two cookies! What a nice fellow," Santa chuckled quietly. He tip-toed over to the counter, took one of the potent treats and popped it in his mouth, chewin' hungrily. Takin' the glass in his other hand, he downed the psychedelic beverage in three big gulps, grabbed the remainin' cookie, and munched on it as he returned to the fireplace. Touchin' a finger to his nose, Santa zipped back up the chimney and popped out the top onto the roof.

A light sprinklin' of snow fell, and a chilly tingle began to form in his chest. Santa stood there for a moment, curiously lookin' at his reindeer as they waited patiently with his sleigh. Rudolph snorted nervously, and his nose lit up. Somethin' wasn't right with ol' Santa Claus.

"Ho...Ho...Um..." Santa began to feel the cool waves radiatin' through his chest and spread slowly through his body. He glanced back at the chimney top, feelin' a tad confused. "How the hell did I manage to fit in there?"

He walked back over to the chimney and peered down the narrow hole into the darkness below. The sooty black interior swirled unsteadily, like a drunken vortex that beckoned the now bewildered Santa back down. He looked again over to his sleigh and the team of wobbly reindeer, then back into the chimney. A multitude of sparkly, colourful lights rushed around inside the seemingly bottomless hole.

His mouth became dry as his head swam in a

sea of disorientation. His teeth felt metallic and jiggled loosely as he ran his pasty-feelin' tongue across them.

"Im-posssss-i-buuhhhhh."

He stood upright and turned once again to his unsettled reindeer.

"What?" he asked abruptly and then looked wildly around as the word *what* echoed in every direction, dancin' 'round his head like a chorus of jeerin', childish…elves?

All the reindeer were worried now, fidgetin' in their harnesses, and glancin' at each other questioningly at Santa's bizarre behaviour. He hoisted his sack back over his shoulder and walked unsteadily to the sleigh. Rudolph and his comrades all turned their heads to watch him climb aboard.

Santa sat there for several moments, starin' off into space as the peak began to take hold. His eyes watered and his bones felt rubbery as he grabbed the reins. Poor ol' Santa didn't know what was goin' on. All he knew was he had deliveries to make and he'd wasted enough time on this roof.

"On Dancer! On Prancer! On Dasher! On

Slasher! ON SMASHER! ON GASHER! ON…ON!...On…on…GAH! Just…ON!!"

Then, with a slap of the jinglin' reins and a boomin' "Ho Ho Ho," the frightened reindeer took their ramblin' master into the night sky. The higher they went, the higher he got. Santa Claus was losin' his marbles at this point and began yellin' unintelligible orders at his reindeer, to which they had no idea how to respond, so they just carried on flyin' whichever slapdash way Santa pulled the reins.

They were meant to be landin' on every roof, but their master was just takin' 'em higher and higher, up through the clouds and headin' into the stratosphere. As they climbed, the air thinned, until at last, Santa completely lost it. His brain became jelly in his skull and his eyes bugged out of his head. His jolly disposition turned to malice, and his reindeer began to get sucked into the maelstrom of his trip, becomin' mentally hooked to Santa's risin' insanity.

"Down!" he ordered, and the reindeer gladly obeyed, takin' the sleigh into a spiralling descent. Rudolph and co. had never had so much fun on their annual jaunt across the world. The stop-start journey across every rooftop was tedious as hell. This was much better. Santa's ramblin' was ceaseless and eventually turned to song. His favourite festive season ditty, Jingle Bells, started to fall from his mouth with a demented, bloody twist...

"Dancing on my clothes, in a one corpse open grave. Through the gates we go, screaming all the way! Aaaaarrrrggghhhhh! Crows on tombstones sing, and make the spirits rise. What fun it is to raise the dead, let's go get some tonight! HO! Demon Bells, ring death knells, boys and girls lie slain. Oh, what fun—it is to hide—in a one corpse open grave, HO! Demon Bells, ring death knells, boys and girls lie slain. Oh, what fun—it is to help—the children die in pain!"

The streets below were near empty as the witchin' hour drew near. Only the odd car movin' slowly along icy roads, and the very occasional person, walkin' quickly to wherever they were headed to escape the freezin' night, were to be seen. Everyone else was tucked warm in their beds, expectin' to wake in the mornin' to a stuffed stocking and a gift littered tree.

Not this year though. Santa Claus was comin' to town, but he was comin' with a vengeance. Brian had turned one of the most beloved characters in history into a screamin', homicidal maniac with his latest and most devastating prank.

For the first time in forever, Santa and his reindeer bypassed the rooftops and touched ground along the main street in town. They tore down the centre of the boulevard at blindin' speed, with Santa whoopin' and hollerin' nightmarish renditions of everybody's favourite Christmas tunes.

A car crawlin' along up ahead began to swerve and slide out of control, as the astonished driver caught sight of the rapidly advancin' chariot of mayhem in his rear vision mirror. Within seconds, Santa and his reindeer caught up, and without breakin' pace, Rudolph and co. leapt over the car with just enough height and distance to allow the sleigh to crash down on top of the roof, before slidin' effortlessly down the front of the vehicle and continuin' on down the road. The car skidded off the road and straight into a pole, leavin' the driver severely whiplashed and stunned beyond belief.

Santa had a sudden change of heart and halted the wildly careenin' sleigh. He decided to go back and help the poor motorist he'd so rudely sent into a pole. Pullin' up on the reins, bells a jinglin', the reindeer performed a splendid backflip pirouette manoeuvre, to land facin' the other way before trottin' casually back to the wrecked car. Santa disembarked and walked up to the broken driver's window.

"Everything okay in there? My apologies for the recklessness of my reindeer. I will be sure to admonish them once we are through here," Santa said slowly, carefully choosin' his words and pushin' 'em out with a concentrated effort to sound sincere.

The driver simply stared at the crazed lookin' Santa, still not believin' what he was lookin' at. Now, if there was one thing Santa could not tolerate, it was rudeness. You always answer when you are spoken to. That's just common courtesy and this driver was showin' him none whatsoever, besides, it's also the height of bad manners to stare.

Santa reached in through the window, mindin' not to tear his sleeve on the jagged glass, and helped himself to a handful of the man's hair. He attempted to pull him out the window but he was still strapped in by his seatbelt, so Santa gave an extra tug to get his head clear of the car. He then proceeded to saw it off at the neck, draggin' it ferociously back 'n' forth along the jagged shards of glass protrudin' up from inside the door. Slivers of window snapped and jutted from the partially severed neck, sprayin' blood in the face of the demented maniac, to match the red of his girth filled outfit.

When the glass had all snapped and wore down, Santa violently shook and pulled the near decapitated noggin until it wrenched free from the neck stump, pullin' the entire length of spine from the spastically convulsin' body.

Finally, the headless corpse slumped inside the car, gushin' torrents of blood into the trashed vehicle's interior. With a triumphant "HO HO HO!" Santa held his trophy aloft, rivulets of blood streamin' from the jagged neck onto both him and the road.

He returned to the sleigh with an evil, beamin' grin. This time, the reindeer weren't worried or confused by their master's behaviour. Instead, they leapt up and down excitedly, slammin' the sleigh against the road repeatedly in a bizarre, jingle-belled Mexican wave. Santa jumped up into his seat with surprisin' agility for his massive frame and plopped the head onto the brake lever in a proud display.

He had now established the end of Christmas cheer to all, and the beginnin' of a rampage of Xmas fear spreadin'. His sanity was well and truly dead. In its place was a newfound enjoyment: one of murder and mayhem that would continue until the night was through.

"You will now refer to me as Sanity Korpse!" he gleefully addressed his jubilant team of reindeer. "HO HO HO! HOOO! HO HO HO HO HO HOOOO!! Onward, you lovely bunch of horny fuckers!"

He slapped a large, bloody gloved hand down on the head and pushed forward, releasin' the brake. Without a moment's hesitation, the empathetically insane Rudolph led the charge upwards and onwards, his ornately red nose bathing the surroundin' air in a crimson glow.

"Next available house, my friends. It's time

we spread some Xmas fear!"

The reindeer obeyed with sadistic pleasure and charged through the air to the nearest rooftop. Sanity Korpse leapt from his perch, landin' on the tiles with an uncustomary loud thud, and headed straight for the chimney. Leapin' high into the air, he performed a graceful swan dive towards the narrow opening, and with a loud "HO!" he disappeared impossibly down the chimney.

Once inside, he made no attempt to be quiet. He hurled his sack across the room, smashin' it into the festively adorned tree and knockin' it to the ground with a violent crash.

Above the fireplace hung three empty stockings and above them, was mounted a shotgun. Sanity Korpse pulled it down from the wall and admired it for a moment. He bounced it up and down in his upturned palms a few times, impressed by its weightiness. He then skipped merrily down the hallway to the first bedroom, whistlin' an Xmas tune.

He was met at the doorway by the father of the house, rudely awakened by the dramatic entrance, and comin' to investigate. Sanity Korpse pointed the shotgun at the startled man and pulled the trigger, but nothin' happened. The damn thing wasn't loaded. The father backed into the bedroom, straight into his wife, who had followed him out of bed to see what all the ruckus was about.

"Well, dig my grave 'n' fuck me!" Sanity Korpse rudely exclaimed. "What use is an unloaded gun? I know!"

He grabbed it by the muzzle in both hands and swung it 'round and over his head in a grossly exaggerated movement, bringin' it down hard onto the father's skull. The wife screamed as her husband went down, the maniac in the bloody red suit bludgeoning him to a pulp.

He looked up at the hysterical woman with a blood-chillin' leer and then swung the shotgun like a baseball bat straight across her terrified face. Blood and teeth flew from her mouth and she slammed against the wall, slumpin' to the floor, dead.

Little eight-year-old William came to the doorway, all bleary eyed until he saw the shockin' scene in his parents' bedroom. His eyes grew wide and his mouth dropped open in a silent scream. Sanity

Korpse turned to face the boy, the same leer painted on his face in William's mummy and daddy's blood.

"It's *waaay* past your bedtime, young man. How very, *very* naughty!"

William turned and ran down the hallway, back to the perceived safety of his bed. He thought maybe, if he were to get back into bed and feign sleep, this terrible waking nightmare would go away. Jumpin' into his bed and pullin' the blankets over his head, he lay there, shiverin' for several seconds in supreme terror.

He wasn't scared for very long. Sanity Korpse burst into the room and proceeded to batter the small, quiverin' lump under the blankets to death, before droppin' the bloody gun to the floor, headin' back out to the fireplace and vanishin' back up the chimney.

Christmas morning was a tragic event that year. Over seventy families were slaughtered in Sanity Korpse's killing spree – and that was only in one town. Reports worldwide, of entire towns massacred, dominated every television channel and radio station. Cities, towns, remote villages on every continent described the same tragedy. The entire world mourned that day, while Sanity Korpse returned home to his clandestine station in the North Pole. Throughout the entire year, he was stuck in his home/prison, until once again a year later, he would be free to resume his murderous rampage across the world. All through that year, Sanity Korpse had ample time to reflect.

Once upon a time, he was content to stay home with Mrs. Claus and his happy workforce of elves. This year however, Mrs. Claus was dismayed by her husband's maniacal return. She wouldn't stop demandin' he tell her what had gone so awry, until he had enough (it didn't take very long – a mere ten minutes in fact) and stormed out of the house to the stables.

Of course, Mrs. Claus followed him, cryin' and pleadin' with him to talk to her. He walked straight up to Donner and snapped off part of his antler. Turnin' to his distraught wife, he then stabbed her repeatedly all over her body until she was still, silent and unrecognisable, then returned to the house to brood for the next twelve months.

Sanity Korpse was entirely miserable in his

insanity; unable to play out his murderous urge, he was confined to his home for what felt like eternity. He recalled back to the moment everythin' changed, when he popped out that chimney and was standin' on Brian's roof. Those cookies were delicious but that milk, as he recalled, had a peculiar taste to it. Had he been poisoned? Was this Brian character out to get him? And where exactly the fuck was that particular house?

He had left his sack at the first household he'd massacred, and that had his enormous list of names and addresses in it. He was gonna get this motherfucker and make him pay. He just had to remember where he lived.

The followin' year was a repeat of the previous, only this time as the night progressed, the violence escalated to entire cities becomin' ghost towns. Sanity Korpse became more and more incensed with each house not bein' his ultimate target, and the more he raged, the more befuddled he became. Before long, he couldn't even recall which country, let alone which house, the elusive Brian resided in.

Many people referred to their once beloved tradition as Stressmas from there on. Families who survived the night never saw any presents. Children the world over would either spend Stressmas day in tears...or dead.

Brian knew he was the cause of this and it played on his mind every wakin' moment, as well as tormentin' his dreams at night. In the meantime, as a penance of sorts, he had decided to clean up his act. No more booze, no more drugs and above all, no more pranks. He threw himself into his work, excellin' at his job, and rose through the ranks to senior vice president of the firm he worked for.

His salary increased greatly in the first year, and Brian took out a loan to buy a secluded holiday cabin in the woods. Here is where he would spend the now defunct holiday season, cowerin' in fear of a Stressmas Eve visit from a vengeful Sanity Korpse.

After five years, the guilt he felt was paramount. Over the years, due to one night a year alone, the world's population had been reduced by two-fifths. Nobody but Brian was aware that this was entirely due to his drug fuelled prank. If anyone were to ever find out the truth, overnight, he would become the most hated – and hunted – man on the planet. Forget Sanity Korpse. His life would be not worth livin' anymore and would be very short lived indeed.

Now it was Stressmas Eve number five, and Brian sat quietly in his log cabin in the woods. The first thing he had done when he bought the joint was brick up the fire place and fill the chimney with cement. It didn't matter that it was freezin' cold, he wasn't takin' any chances. His annual ritual of sittin' in the middle of the livin' room, dressed in his thermals and several layers of clothes, wrapped in thick blankets, provided for a very silent night.

Tearin' across the night sky, Sanity Korpse traversed oceans, mountain ranges, deserts, forests and plains; stoppin' in every town, village and city to exact his indiscriminate revenge. Rudolph all of a sudden halted the sleigh mid-air.

"What is it, Rudolph?" Sanity Korpse asked. The reindeer turned his head back to stare imploringly at his master, his red nose glowin' furiously, and then turned his gaze downwards to the town below.

"Brian?"

In reply, Rudolph began a hurried descent in a bee line for one roof in particular. As they got nearer, that same icy chill hit Sanity Korpse mercilessly in the chest, spreadin' through him like a ravenous virus. He recognized that roof beyond any shadow of a doubt, and he slapped the reins with a burst of bloodthirsty excitement.

"Rudolph, you splendid beast! I could kiss you! Downward! Faster, faster, faster!"

They hit the roof without slowin', crashin' into the explodin' tiles with enough force to send several broken pieces rocketin' through the windows of the house across the street. No sooner had they landed, Sanity Korpse bounded from the sleigh and disappeared down the chimney. While the reindeer waited on the roof impatiently, they heard a howl of rage from inside the house. Sanity Korpse ran from room to empty room, tearin' the place apart – then there was silence.

Rudolph and co. listened intently above while inside, Sanity Korpse stood with that evil grin, holdin' a piece of paper in his hands: It was the deed to the cabin in the woods. With a violent flick of his nose, Sanity Korpse whooshed up the chimney, sailed through the air and landed directly in front of Rudolph. With wide, bulbous eyes and an ear-to-ear grin, he shoved the paper in Rudolph's face.

"We have found him, my dear friends!" he almost screamed.

He did a crazy little dance and shoved the paper back in Rudolph's face, then whirled around three times on the spot before jumpin' back to his seat. Grabbin' the skull, with random leathery strips of flesh still clingin' here 'n' there, he slammed the brake lever forward and they were off. The cabin was a mere thirty miles away and they were there before you could say *festive.*

Brian was noddin' off when suddenly his silent night was unceremoniously shattered.

He jumped to his feet and his stomach leapt into his throat at the deafening crash on the roof. Any other night of the year, he would've guessed a tree had fallen on the house, but not this night. He knew exactly what the noise above was, and he pissed his pants with fear at the sound of heavy footsteps runnin' across his roof, stoppin' directly above the fireplace. There were a few tense moments of silence then two heavy steps towards the edge of the roof, followed by the loud crunch of somethin' landin' in the snow outside. Then he heard him.

"*Briiiiaaaannn!   Bbbbbrrriiiiaaaaaannnnn!* Ho fucking Ho Ho Ho!"

Brian felt the blood drain from his face, then his body, settlin' in his legs and rootin' him to the spot as the madman outside circled around the cabin towards the front door, rappin' his knuckles on the log walls as he went.

Brian followed the sound of his doom along the wall with his eyes. His heart skipped a beat as Sanity Korpse rounded the corner to the front side of the cabin. A shadow was cast across the window, and Brian trembled uncontrollably, fallin' to the floor as his legs gave way.

Sanity Korpse stared at him through the window, his face a beamin' picture of psychosis as he waved to Brian emphatically, like a long distant relative returnin' home after years away. Brian was sittin', but his feet hadn't moved from their spot on the floor. He was paralysed with terror at the vision he beheld outside the window. It was too late when he noticed the steel bar leanin' against the wall next to the front door. He had forgotten to slide it across the door to brace it, but there was nothin' he could do about that now.

Sanity Korpse gave a polite knock on the door, sendin' waves of nausea up and down Brian's torso.

"*Briiiiaaaannnn...Bri   Bri   Briiiiiaaannn!* Aren't you going to let me in? It's cold out here, y'know? Brian?"

"N-No! G-g-Go away!"

"Oh, Brian. That's not very charitable of you. It's Christmas! Where's your holiday spirit? C'mon, just open the door. I brought milk 'n' cookies to share."

That last statement and the sing-song way in which it was delivered made Brian throw up. It didn't matter that the rest of the world didn't know about his stunt. The rest of the world weren't here right now, but this crazy fat man in the red suit was, and he wanted revenge.

"Please, just go away. Leave! I'm not opening

the door. Not tonight. Not ever!" Brian's wailin' plea was met with a more vigorous *thump-thump-thump* on the solid wooden door.

"C'mon, Brian. It'll be so much easier if you just open the door. Do you want me to freeze to death out here? …Brian?"

Brian didn't respond nor did he move from his position on the floor.

"BRIAN!" Sanity Korpse screamed and began to pound rapidly on the door with both fists, and then with his shoulder.

Sanity Korpse was strong, but the solid oak door was apparently stronger. Nonetheless, Brian pissed himself a second time, still unable to move and unwillin' to say another word. He just hoped the mad man would give up and go away. Sanity Korpse had waited a long time and searched for Brian far and wide, however. He wasn't goin' anywhere without first takin' five years of frustration and insanity out on the man inside. He wanted closure. Sanity Korpse wanted revenge!

The assault on the door ceased, and Brian held his breath until he could hear his heart thumpin' in his ears. He strained to hear above his poundin' heart and for a moment, hoped that maybe he had indeed given up and left.

His hopes shattered along with the window as Sanity Korpse suddenly appeared, divin' head first through the glass and gettin' wedged, halfway in. His huge belly prevented him from squeezin' through as he struggled and wriggled unsuccessfully over the kitchen sink. All the while, he glared at Brian with a painted-on smile, and eyes that betrayed the smile as a murderous smirk. His magic only worked on rooftops. Windows and doors were a different story altogether.

Brian saw his chance and willed his legs to obey him, jumpin' to his feet and runnin' to the door to retrieve the heavy steel bar. Pickin' it up, he rushed to the maniac in his window and swung the bar with all his might onto the mad man's head.

"Don't do that," Sanity Korpse said with a casual air.

Brian hit him again, but Sanity Korpse just looked at him and chuckled with amusement.

"Don't be silly now, Brian. You can't kill

Sanity Korpse!"

Desperately, Brian brought the solid steel down again and again, but Sanity Korpse just laughed at him as he continued to struggle his way in through the window. It was slow goin' but he was inchin' his way through, bit by bit, as Brian continued his frantic, but useless, assault.

"You do know you're only making things worse for yourself. You should've just opened the door and this would all be over now."

Brian dropped the bar and backed away in tears of frustration and despair, at the calm, unruffled tone of the maniac's voice. After the beatin' he'd just given him, by all rights, he should be dead, but no. He continued to squeeze his massive body through the window, slowly but surely.

Brian was almost hysterical with panic and then the thought struck. Without wastin' another moment, he rushed to the door and flung it open, runnin' outside and headin' for the trees, while his would-be killer remained jammed in the window.

Brian was not out of the woods yet though. He heard a whoosh of air behind him and a shadow fell over him, followed by bells ringin' and hooves slappin' into the snow-covered ground. Brian turned just in time to see the insane reindeer chargin' him down, and he fell onto his back with his hands up, coverin' his face.

The massive deer with the glowin' red nose stomped on Brian's legs and kicked him square in the balls. Brian screamed out in pain, answered by Rudolph's antler flippin' him over onto his stomach and continuin' to stomp on his legs and back, while the other reindeer spurred him on. Every time Brian tried to curl up or cover himself with his arms, Rudolph would lay him out flat with his antlers and continue kickin' the shit out of him.

One solid hoof to the side of Brian's head brought his terrified struggle to an end. Brian was knocked the fuck out. Both his legs were broken in several places as well as many of his ribs, as Brian lay out cold on the snow, bleedin' from the wound to his skull.

By now, Sanity Korpse had managed to squeeze all the way through the window and had run outside again just in time to see Brian fall still. He slowed to a triumphant march towards his foe and his trusty team of reindeer. The leerin' grin still plastered on his face.

"Nice work, Rudolph! Shall we take Brian home now? I think the poor fellow has suffered enough, don't you?"

All of the other reindeer looked bewildered at the apparent change of heart, but Rudolph knew better. He stepped forward and lowered his head, scoopin' the broken, unconscious Brian up in his antlers, then with a powerful flick, tossed him through the air like a rag doll back over the reindeers' heads onto the sleigh. With a hearty "HO HO HO!" Sanity Korpse jumped up into his seat and away they went.

They flew circles around Brian's house for nearly two hours before he regained consciousness. The freezin' cold wind blasted his face, and his broken bones screamed at him while his body shivered uncontrollably.

"You're awake!" Sanity Korpse said with a laugh. "We're taking you home, Brian, but first I want to take you to a special place. Up we go!"

With a slap of the reins, Rudolph and the team

of reindeer began their steep ascent. Brian didn't speak. His tongue was stiff in his mouth, and his teeth chattered painfully as higher and higher they went.

"That was a fine prank you played on ol' Santa Claus way back when," Sanity Korpse said to Brian in friendly conversation. Brian didn't reply. "I'm going to take you to the place where your prank changed my life first, and then you can go home. Our business will be concluded."

Relief flooded Brian at these words. Sanity Korpse was speakin' to him in a pleasant tone and it seemed he was goin' to survive this encounter after all. As the sleigh climbed higher and broke through the clouds, his relief was corrupted by severe dizziness and his broken ribs made breathin' the icy thin air unbearable, yet higher they went until finally they stopped.

Sanity Korpse felt the familiar sensation in his chest and knew this was the exact spot his mind had snapped. He reached behind and grabbed Brian by the shoulder, haulin' him over to the seat beside him. The agony in Brian's body made him want to scream, but at the same time prevented him from doin' so.

"This is it, Brian. This is the exact place where ol' Santa Claus lost his mind. Maybe you could find it for me?"

Brian looked nervously at the maniac by his side, but couldn't speak. He was shiverin' too hard and his head swam in agony. He felt he too was beginnin' to lose his mind, and then a shock charged through his entire being. Sanity Korpse had flung him over the side of the sleigh, and he was now free fallin' towards the clouds below.

He opened his mouth to scream, but it was filled with an impossible blast of freezing wind. All he could do was choke as he fell. The wind roared in his ears and he didn't hear the jingle bells or the "Ho Ho Ho."

Another shock jolted his body as the reindeer shot past him, followed by the mad man on the sleigh. They were tauntin' him in his death plummet, flyin' circles around him as he fell.

Breakin' through the clouds, Brian saw the landscape far below gettin' gradually closer with each passin' second. Faster and faster he descended, gravity cruelly beckonin' him to his doom. He wanted to pass out but couldn't. He wanted to be back home, but not this way.

As the abstract shapes below began to take on more recognisable forms, Brian started to accept his fate. He had caused the deaths of millions of people with a single, stupid idea, and now he was payin' the ultimate price. He realised he deserved it and resigned himself to his own death.

He had made peace with his maker and with himself. Now he just wanted it to be over. He closed his eyes and let his mind wander; driftin' on the wind gently, instead of his real predicament of plummetin' at a ridiculous velocity.

He didn't get to wander far, and he didn't even make it home. Brian missed his house completely and splattered on the road out front.

At the very instant Brian's life came to an end, a loud snap, audible even to the reindeer, went off inside Sanity Korpse's head and Santa Claus returned.

There were no presents that Stressmas, but nobody else died at the hands of the fat man in the red suit. The followin' year, people the world over returned to their homes after hidin' throughout

Stressmas Eve, to find an abundance of presents piled neatly where they used to place their tree. Sanity Korpse was gone and Christmas had returned.

Many fangs to you all and congratulations on making it through in one piece! If you enjoyed this little romp and haven't come through too traumatised, be sure to check out my first little collection of flash fiction tales of terror and torment – FLASH OF DARKNESS

https://www.amazon.com/Flash-Darkness-Toneye-Eyenot-ebook/dp/B079DHTH41/

and stay tuned for many more from Luniakk Publications. We're only just gettin' warmed up!

The morbid pleasure has been all '*ours*'

~ Toneye/Eyenot

FLASH OF DARKNESS

TONEYE EYENOT

LUNARIK PUBLICATIONS

ABOUT THE AUTHOR

Toneye Eyenot writes tales of horror and dark fantasy which have appeared in dozens of anthologies over the past four years.

He is the author of WOLVZ: WHISPERS OF WAR, a novella as part of J. Ellington Ashton's PROJECT 26, a clown/werewolf horror novella titled BLOOD MOON BIG TOP, released with JEA Press, plus the ongoing SACRED BLADE OF PROFANITY series with two books, THE SCARLETT CURSE and JOSHUA'S FOLLY, also published through J. Ellington Ashton Press, plus a third instalment currently in the works.

He is the editor of the anthologies: VAMPZ VZ WOLVZ, DANCE WITH THE DEMON, INSECTILE ILLUSION, PSYCHO PATH, BLACK MAGIC MASSACRE, FULL MOON SLAUGHTER werewolf anthology, and FULL MOON SLAUGHTER 2: ALTERED BEASTS, all with JEA. Toneye lurks in the Blue Mountains in NSW Australia, with the myriad voices who tear the horrors from his mind and splatter them onto the page.

You can most easily connect with Toneye through his Facebook page:
https://www.facebook.com/Toneye-Eyenot-Dark-Author-Musician-1128293857187537/
Or website:
http://luniakkpublications.wordpress.com
Amazon: https://www.amazon.com/Toneye-Eyenot/e/B00NVVMHVA/
Twitter: **https://twitter.com/ToneyeEyenot**
G+: **https://plus.google.com/u/0/+toneyeeyenot**
Instagram:
https://www.instagram.com/toneyeblakk/
Pinterest: **https://www.pinterest.com.au/eyenot/**

ABOUT THE ARTIST

Mar G-A. is a woman of many talents – artist, author, book promoter, reviewer, and compulsive thinker. She is the founder and owner of The Bold Mom – a place where you will find a vast world of horrific delights, from interviews, reviews, dark poetry, stories, exciting and disturbing projects, links to several other great sites promoting Horror in its various forms...and the list goes on. You will get lost in the world she has built there, and happily so.

Mar – and The Bold Mom – are a swiftly rising force in the indie Horror community, offering an exemplary service and invaluable support to many authors as well as publishers. You can find her all over social media, whether you are an author looking for help with pushing your work, or a reader, ravenous for new Horrors to sink your fangs into.

Website: http://www.theboldmom.com/
Art Portfolio: https://art.tt/3gfx
Facebook: (The Bold Mom):
https://www.facebook.com/theboldmom/
(Mar G-A.):
https://www.facebook.com/disturbing.drawings/
Twitter: https://twitter.com/theboldmom
Instagram:
https://www.instagram.com/theboldmom/
G+: https://plus.google.com/u/0/+TheBoldMom
Pinterest:
https://www.pinterest.com.au/theboldmom/

30771477R00069

Printed in Poland
by Amazon Fulfillment
Poland Sp. z o.o., Wrocław